Rock 'n' Roll Mole

Carolyn Crimi
pictures by
Lynn Munsinger

SCHOLASTIC INC.

To Mick, Bono, Bruce, and Dad
—C.C.

For my cousins Alex, Kendall, and Lara. They rock!
—LM.

ISBN 978-0-545-54247-0

12 11 10 9 8 7 6 5 4 3 2 1   13 14 15 16 17 18/0

Printed in the U.S.A.   40

First Scholastic printing, April 2013

Designed by Nancy R. Leo-Kelly
Text set in Clichee

The art was rendered on Saunders Waterford watercolor paper
with watercolors, pen and ink, and colored pencil.

Mole had a rock-and-roll soul.
He woke up each morning yelling,

"Let's rock the house!"

He wore a leather jacket (even in summer)

and shades (even at night).

And he could strut just like his idol, Mick Badger.

At school three chicks followed him around. They screamed
"Oooo, Mole!" in their tweety voices.

"Your jacket is so cool!" his best friend Pig often told him.

"I love your shades!" Raccoon always said.

Oh yeah, Mole had style all right.
When he was alone he could
strut, snarl, and play guitar like a legend.

But the thought of performing in front of
others made him shake in his shades.

Pig was the only one who had ever heard him play.

"You're **awesome!**" Pig said.
"You should play in front of the whole school!"

Mole didn't say anything. It was one thing to play in front of Pig.
But the whole school? No way.

Pig already had an idea, though. He wanted to put on a talent show. Raccoon could torch the crowd with his extreme skateboard stunts.

The chicks would rip it up with
their sweet songbird voices.

Pig knew some smooth dance moves——he positively sizzled.

And Mole? Everybody knew
what he should do.

"You'll rule the stage with your guitar!" said Pig.
"Um, yeah," said Mole. "It'll be platinum."

"Oooo, Mole! You're really going to play for us?"

All three chicks fainted on the spot.

But that night Mole worried.
He stared at his posters of Moo 2 and Goose Springsteen.
"What if I'm no good?" he wondered.

But they were, like, just posters, so they couldn't answer him.

The next morning Mole got up early to practice.

He tried strumming
his guitar,
but his paws shook.

He tried strutting
across his room,
but his legs wobbled.

He tried **screaming** out a song, but his voice cracked.

At school the chicks cried "Oooo, Mole!" but he barely heard them.
They swooned, and he stepped right over them.

Before he went to sleep that night, Mole stashed his
leather jacket and his shades under his bed.
He even took down his posters.

"I'm not going to do Pig's stupid show," he mumbled. "I quit."

The next day, Mole broke the news to Pig.

Pig's tail uncurled. "You have to do it! We've already told everyone!"

Mole shrugged. "Sorry," he said. "I just can't."

"Can you at least help me get everything ready?" Pig asked.

"Okay," said Mole. "But I'm not playing. No way."

Mole and Pig worked on the show every day after school.
They sold tickets to all the animals in town.

"I hope everything goes okay," Pig said.
"Just hang loose," Mole said. "It'll be platinum, dude."

But the night of the show, Pig was sweating more than usual.
"My iPod is broken! I don't have any music!
How am I supposed to dance?"
Mole looked at his best friend's worried face.
He knew what he should do. "I'll be right back," he said.

Mole ran to his house and got his guitar. He put on his shades and his leather jacket.

"Just hang loose," he told himself. But when he pictured the audience, he started to shake.
Then he thought of Pig, and he gave himself a rattle.
Finally, he was ready to roll.

Pig's face brightened when he saw Mole.
"I knew you'd come through!"

PIG'S
TALENT

From backstage Mole and Pig watched
until it was their turn.

"Let's give it up for Mole and Pig!"
cried Raccoon.

SHOW

Mole jumped onto the stage. He tried
to swagger. He stumbled. Then he fell.

The audience stared.
Mole stared back.

I'm doomed, he thought.
"Hang loose!" whispered Pig.

Mole gulped.
He took a deep breath.

Then he sprang back up and struck a pose.

"LET'S ROCK THE HOUSE!"

Mole cranked.
He burned.

He scorched the stage
with his fierce, funky sounds.

"OOOO, MOLE!!"
screamed the chicks.

He strutted and snarled,
ripped and roared.

He played and sang like the
supersonic, groovelicious
rock star that he was,

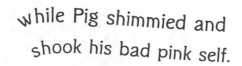

while Pig shimmied and
shook his bad pink self.

Everyone clapped and stomped and screamed when
Mole and Pig took their bows.

"We really showed them who's boss," said Pig.

Mole smiled. "Pig, we were pure platinum."